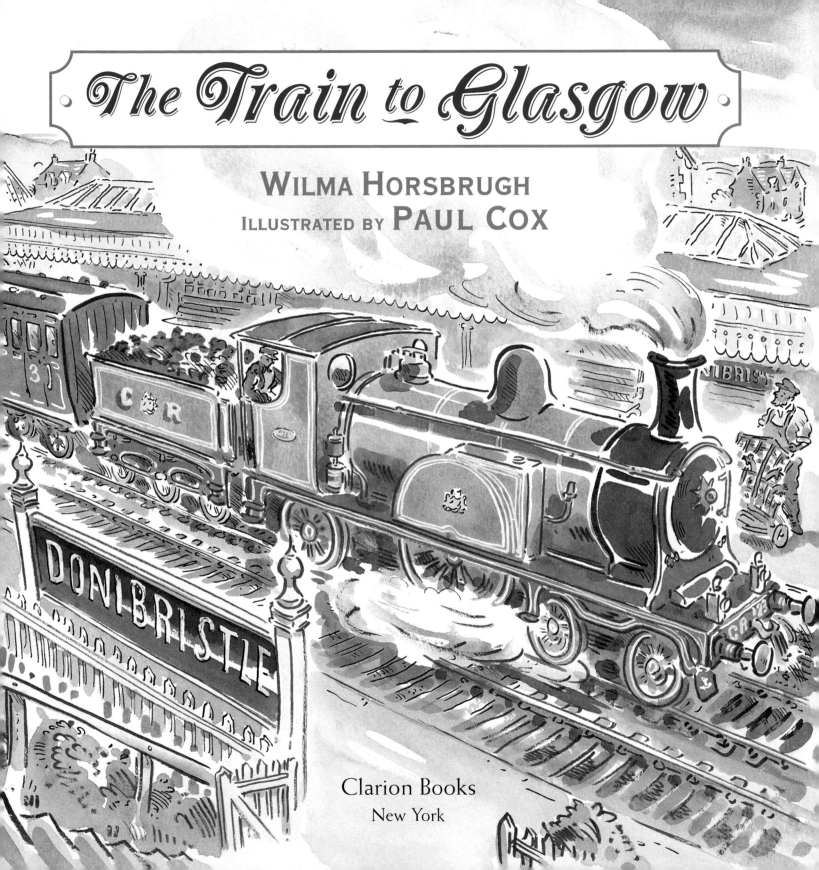

The Train to Glasgow

WILMA HORSBRUGH

ILLUSTRATED BY PAUL COX

Clarion Books

New York

For Jack Cox

Clarion Books
a Houghton Mifflin Company imprint
215 Park Avenue South, New York, NY 10003

Published in the United States in 2004 by arrangement with
The Albion Press Ltd., Spring Hill, Idbury, Oxfordshire OX7 6RU, England

Text copyright 1954 by Wilma Horsbrugh
Illustrations copyright © 2004 by Paul Cox

"The Train to Glasgow" was first published in *Clinkerdump and Other Stories in Rhyme*
(London: Methuen, 1954) and is reprinted by kind permission of Marian Horsbrugh.

Designed by Emma Bradford

The illustrations were executed in watercolor on paper.
The text was set in 15-point Weiss Bold.

For information about permission to reproduce selections from this book, write to
Permissions, Houghton Mifflin Company, 215 Park Avenue South, New York, NY 10003.

www.houghtonmifflinbooks.com

Library of Congress Cataloging-in-Publication Data

Horsbrugh, Wilma.
  The train to Glasgow / by Wilma Horsbrugh ; illustrated by Paul Cox.
    p. cm.
Summary: A rhyme in the style of "The House That Jack Built," describing
the antics that occur when some chickens get loose on a train bound for
Glasgow.
  ISBN 0-618-38143-0
  [1. Railroads–Trains–Fiction. 2. Stories in rhyme.] I. Cox, Paul,
ill. II. Title.
  PZ8.3.H7874Tr 2004
  [E]–dc22   2003012200

10 9 8 7 6 5 4 3 2 1

Typesetting: Servis Filmsetting Ltd, Manchester
Color origination: Classicscan, Singapore
Printed in Hong Kong/China by South China Printing Co.

Here is the train to Glasgow.

Here is the driver,
Mr. MacIver,
Who drove the train to Glasgow.

Here is the guard from Donibristle,
Who waved his flag and blew his whistle
To tell the driver,
Mr. MacIver,
To start the train to Glasgow.

Here is a boy called Donald MacBrain,
Who came to the station to catch the train

But saw the guard from Donibristle
Wave his flag and blow his whistle
To tell the driver,
Mr. MacIver,
To start the train to Glasgow.

Here is the guard, a kindly man,
Who, at the last moment, hauled into the van
That fortunate boy called Donald MacBrain,
Who came to the station to catch the train
But saw the guard from Donibristle
Wave his flag and blow his whistle
To tell the driver,
Mr. MacIver,
To start the train to Glasgow.

Here are hens and here are cocks,
Clucking and crowing inside a box,
In charge of the guard, that kindly man,
Who, at the last moment, hauled into the van
That fortunate boy called Donald MacBrain,
Who came to the station to catch the train

But saw the guard from Donibristle
Wave his flag and blow his whistle
To tell the driver,
Mr. MacIver,
To start the train to Glasgow.

Here is the train. It gave a jolt,
Which loosened a catch and loosened a bolt,
And let out the hens and let out the cocks,
Clucking and crowing out of their box,
In charge of the guard, that kindly man,
Who, at the last moment, hauled into the van

That fortunate boy called Donald MacBrain,
Who came to the station to catch the train
But saw the guard from Donibristle
Wave his flag and blow his whistle
To tell the driver,
Mr. MacIver,
To start the train to Glasgow.

The guard chased a hen and, missing it, fell.

The hens were all squawking, the cocks were as well,
And unless you were there, you haven't a notion
The flurry, the fuss, the noise and commotion

Caused by the train, which gave a jolt
And loosened a catch and loosened a bolt
And let out the hens and let out the cocks,
Clucking and crowing out of their box,

In charge of the guard, that kindly man,
Who, at the last moment, hauled into the van
That fortunate boy called Donald MacBrain,
Who came to the station to catch the train

But saw the guard from Donibristle
Wave his flag and blow his whistle
To tell the driver,
Mr. MacIver,
To start the train to Glasgow.

Now Donald was quick and Donald was neat
And Donald was nimble on his feet.

He caught the hens and he caught the cocks
And he put them back in their great big box.

The guard was pleased as pleased could be
And invited Donald to come to tea
On Saturday, at Donibristle,
And let him blow his lovely whistle,
And said in all his life he'd never
Seen a boy so quick and clever.

And so did the driver,
Mr. MacIver,
Who drove the train to Glasgow.

DATE DUE